Horses

and

Moore

By Kay Woodhouse

PublishAmerica
Baltimore

© 2008 by Kay Woodhouse.
All rights reserved. No part of this book may be reproduced, stored in a retrieval system or transmitted in any form or by any means without the prior written permission of the publishers, except by a reviewer who may quote brief passages in a review to be printed in a newspaper, magazine or journal.

First printing

All characters in this book are fictitious, and any resemblance to real persons, living or dead, is coincidental.

PublishAmerica has allowed this work to remain exactly as the author intended, verbatim, without editorial input.

ISBN: 1-60610-675-9
PUBLISHED BY PUBLISHAMERICA, LLLP
www.publishamerica.com
Baltimore

Printed in the United States of America

*Dedicated to
My granddaughters,
Mandy, Allie, Samantha and Sarah
Who all love horses.*

Table of Contents

Chapter One: All About Me and the Deal 9

Chapter Two: All About the Camp 12

Chapter Three: Who's Who 15

Chapter Four: Duties, Classes and Free Time 18

Chapter Five: Dinner and the Staff 24

Chapter Six: The Beginning 29

Chapter Seven: Stables and Tack 35

Chapter Eight: Camping Skills 41

Chapter Nine: Riding 46

Chapter Ten: Chuck Wagons and Hayrides 53

Chapter Eleven: The Caves 63

Chapter Twelve: The Final Days 72

Horses
and
Moore

Chapter One
All About Me and the Deal

Grandma and I made a deal. She would pay my way to camp and I would help her do her 'deep cleaning' in the spring. I am Shawn Ashley Moore, better known as Sam, and I am 12 years old. I've just been promoted to 7th grade, and I am a girl. Both of my names could be for a boy, and I honestly think that my parents wanted a boy—had that name picked out, and decided to use it anyway, even if I was a girl. Of course *they* have never admitted to this, but that's what I think, anyway. I also have two brothers and one sister. My brothers, Cody and Cameron, are nine and six, respectively. Shannon, the family pride and joy is two. The boys and I all look pretty much alike. We have straight, auburn hair, freckles and we're all tall and gangly. Then there is Shannon—even at two she is a beauty. She has blond, curly hair, blue eyes, and dimples. We all love her because there is just no reason not to. She's not even spoiled, even though the boys and I try.

My mom and dad are typical for parents. My dad is a Director in his company. He's in charge of the accounting department. Mom is a Realtor for the Morrison Real Estate agency in our town. They're okay parents. Yes, they keep after me to do my homework, make my bed and household chores, keep track of my sister and brothers, ground me if I don't and reward me with a weekly allowance if I do okay. Typical, I guess, at least when my girlfriends and I compare notes. It seems we all suffer from the same kinds of stuff. But hey, I'm not complaining. I really like my life.

Anyhow, to get back to my deal with Grandma, she had all sorts of projects for me to do, and all through April and May, on Saturday mornings, I rode my bike over to Grandma's. We had a great time working together. You might think it was boring, but it wasn't.

I polished all of her silver dishes and the coffee service, all her good silverware and the water pitcher one time. Another time we vacuumed out all the chairs and furniture in the house, plus turned over all the mattresses and vacuumed the beds, and under them. One weekend we got the garden all spaded up and planted her vegetables and flowers.

The next weekend we cleaned cupboards. We took everything out. Then we washed all the dishes, glasses, cups, saucers, plates, everything that was in there, plus the cupboards with the spices, baking stuff, cereals and all that kind of food. After we washed all those shelves we had to put all the stuff back in neatly.

It went on like this for nine weeks, but now I have paid for one week at Camp Weemo in Tyler, Kentucky. This is a *horse camp* and Grandma knows of my passion for horses.

I continued to go over to my grandparents' house each Saturday through June, too, just because it gave me some special time with them. Grandpa found things for me to do, too, which I really enjoyed. One Saturday we just went fishing and I even hooked the worms on myself. I'm not sure it was a successful fishing day for him, because we only caught a few fish, but I got a huge crappie and they are my favorites. Grandma fried them up and they were so delicious. I ate supper over there that night. Grandma and Grandpa are games and cards people, so whenever we are there we always have a good time.

Chapter Two
All About the Camp

A number of years ago Grandma read an article about Camp Weemo in one of her AARP magazines. Actually they were recruiting retired cooks, teachers, nurses and administrators to establish the camp. Being the pack rat that she is she saved a follow up article on the camp. She shared it with me last Christmas Eve. "If you want to check this camp out, you might find it's something you would want to do," Grandma said, as she handed me the article. At that point nothing was said about 'our deal' which would come up later.

"Thanks, Grandma. I think I will." I did do some investigating on the computer, letter writing and such and found out about the camp. The more I read the more I wanted to be able to go.

Camp Weemo was established in 1995 by a group of retired

businessmen as an opportunity for city kids to learn all about horses on an honest-to-goodness plantation in Tyler, Kentucky. The weekly maximum was 16 kids at a cost of $270.00 per week. The age limit was 10-15 years old. Six hundred forty acres of Kentucky Blue Grass…it sounded like Heaven to me The plantation consisted of a large southern home, a stable of 24 horses, the outbuildings necessary on a plantation, a tennis court, a swimming pool, a recreation building, and the caretakers' homes.

There were two kids per room with one counselor for every four kids. Classes were to be scheduled on horseback riding, grooming of the horses, training horses, various equestrian skills, with swimming, tennis, archery and overnights as well.

The meals were served in the large formal dining room with the dinner meal at night being a dress-up occasion. That meant no shorts, cutoffs or jeans. Bummer. Skorts were acceptable—thank heavens.

The campers were instructed to arrive by 3:00 P.M. on the Sunday of their week, and be picked up by 10:00 A.M. on the following Saturday. A shuttle service would be provided to transport campers to and from the airport, 27 miles away in Lexington.

Armed with all this information, Grandma and I were able

to convince my folks that this was a worthwhile, educational opportunity for me. Plus with me working and with Grandpa and Grandma paying, it seemed fine. I knew I could earn my spending money from the babysitting jobs I had.

We sent in my registration in February, and in March I had a letter back accepting me as a camper. I was selected as one of 12 visiting campers for the week of July 10-16, 2005.

Along with my acceptance letter were the Rules and Regulations…stated very clearly. There was also another sheet listing the clothing we needed for the week, a list of supplies we were expected to bring with us and a list of the kids scheduled for that week. The roommates were highlighted and we were encouraged to write to our roommate between March and June so we'd get to know them a little before we arrived in July. I was scheduled to room with a Janis Esker. I also wrote to a Hannah Goldsmith, just because I like to write letters, and I like the name Hannah, and she lives in Wisconsin.

Chapter Three
Who's Who

The trip to Camp Weemo was a typical flight to Tyler, Kentucky. We were met at the airport by a driver holding a big placard with "Camp Weemo" in huge letters. A couple of the kids I had seen on the flight gravitated to the guy with the sign, so I did too. He had a clipboard with twelve names on it, and asked each of us our name and checked us off. I've always had a good memory for names and I recognized them from our first letter. Janis Esker wasn't there yet, but Hannah Goldsmith was, as were Josh Cummins, Kenny Stegge, and Alex Skuzinski. The rest were still to come. That was the roster for our week at Camp Weemo. As it turned out, the five of us who arrived first were from the Midwest. Iowa, Minnesota and Wisconsin. The rest who were to arrive shortly on the next two flights were from New York, North Carolina and Florida. Six states and twelve kids…I wondered if there was any reason for the numbers. That's how my mind works. I love to solve problems and I always try to figure out stuff. Not that I always do, mind you, but I get a charge out of trying. I love a challenge. I immediately gravitated to Hannah, as she and I were the only girls in the group. I was glad that she and I had exchanged a couple of letters 'cause I felt as if we knew each other a little. She had told me that her roommate was Alissa Forsythe, so we were eager for Janis and Alissa to get there.

The guys were standing around sizing each other up. From my point of view they seemed like typical guys. The one named Josh looked like a cool kid. He had a neat smile, too. They looked to be about the same age as Hannah and me. Although, maybe fourteen or so 'cause they're as tall as we were. So many of the boys in my class at school were shrimps. Mom keeps telling me that they'll grow, just give them a couple of years. She also said that I was probably as tall as I was going to get. I was already five foot six, and Hannah seemed about the same. It's a girl thing, I guess, to grow faster than the guys at this point in our lives.

Our driver was Darrel and he seemed really nice. He gave us badges with our names and was telling us about all the neat activities we were going to get to do. He said, "You kids will each have chores that you'll be responsible for and classes to attend. You'll also have a free time each day to use as you want." It was a scheduled free time and not necessarily the same time each day, or at the same time as our roommates. That sounded good to me, as I figured we all could use some private time when we could do whatever we wanted.

The next two flights came in and all of a sudden there were twelve of us all piling into this shuttle bus that Darrel was driving. All our luggage was collected and stowed away and we were all talking non-stop on the twenty-seven mile trip to the camp. Darrel had seated us in a special order, we discovered. Non-Roomies together with two from other teams right across the aisle. It was a good way to get acquainted.

Darrel said there were four long term campers who would be with us during the week. They were administrators' grandkids who spent the summer at the camp. Alissa Forsythe, Hannah's roommate, was one of them. That gave us a total of eight girls and eight guys for the week. I had wondered why the first letter had said twelve campers instead of sixteen, but I guessed it really didn't make that much difference. We were going to have a great week.

Long termers were divided up between the teams. Each team was assigned to one counselor. The girls had a girl counselor, and the guys, a guy. Made sense to me. Our counselor's name was Karen Lawson. They were all college kids who had been former campers of Camp Weemo. Since the camp wasn't that old I figured they had to have been some of the first campers. I could hardly wait to get started.

Chapter Four
Duties, Classes and Free Time

Our counselor, Karen, rounded up the four girls of our team together and herded us, with all our gear, to our rooms. Janis and I were in one room and Alissa and Hannah were right next to us, with an adjoining door between. There were three single beds in each room. Karen quickly cleared that up by saying, "I split my nights between the two rooms. If you need me or anything at all I will be in one bed or the other, never far away.

"Now get your gear all squared away in the dresser or closet and remember that I have space in there, too."

Janis chose the middle drawer, and I took the bottom one. I would have much rather have had the top one which was Karen's—but, oh, it really didn't matter.

"As soon as you girls are all unpacked come on back in here and I'll go over some of the things you need to know about the camp," Karen said. She turned and walked down the hall to the bathroom.

It didn't take long to unpack and stash my stuff in *my* drawer, on the bottom. My golly, I am five foot six and Janis is probably all of four foot ten. There goes Mom's theory of a girl being as tall as she'll be at twelve. Janis had a long way to go, as far as I was concerned. Anyhow, she should have the bottom drawer. But I'm not complaining. You won't hear me whining about the bottom drawer anymore. I promise.

I bet we all got unpacked and settled in record time, because Karen was just coming down the hall as Hannah and Alissa were coming through our door. "Okay, ladies. Listen up, 'cause I'm going to go through this fast and only one time. Got that?"

"Yeah," we all chorused, like we'd been practicing. We were really curious about just what Karen was going to tell us. We had all read the pamphlets, and Darrel had already given us a crash course on the way to the camp. So what more was there?

"All the kids at this camp are really special people. You, too, you know. The four all summer campers are grandkids of administrators or staff. Each year they apply for one of their grandkids to be able to attend. Of course they have to be the right age, and they can only come once. It really works out okay. The four of them are split up between the weekly campers, and Alissa is ours this week."

We all took a look at Alissa. She was another little one and she was going to be able to tell us what to do?

"She will be your guide this week in case you can't find some place or you have any questions. She's been with us for five weeks already and is really a trooper. She might be a tiny girl, but she is thirteen and knows the ropes around here."

I was the giant of the group. No question about it.

"I have your schedules and after we're done here you can look them over and make sure you understand everything."

"There is a duty schedule and you are each assigned a chore for every day. It is your responsibility to make sure you get it done. You have two breaks during the day, and use one of them for your chore for that day, if you need to."

"What if we get done before the next class?" I said.

"Then you have some free time.

"The day you're on K. P. you go to the kitchen an hour before each meal and help prepare that day's meals. You are excused from whatever class you have scheduled for that time. It will be either fishing or canoeing. Everyone has at least three classes of each of those."

"So the other classes are the ones about the horses?" I asked.

"Yes, the other classes are grooming and brushing, care of the stables and the tack, learning riding techniques and skills, and then just riding. Every day you will have those classes.

There also are classes on Camping Skills. For your break time you can go to the swimming pool, play tennis, do archery, write letters, read books, or do nothing if you want.

"Every night from seven 'til eight forty-five we all get together around the campfire. We share things that are happening, sing songs, tell stories, do skits and that kind of stuff. It's a 'calm down' time before we go to bed.

"There will be eight kids in your classes, but not the same eight in each class. Does that make sense to you? See, in riding class there will be seven other kids, and you eight will always be together in your riding class. But in skills class, you'll be with seven other kids. Oh, of course there will be one or two in each class that were in another class. After all there are only sixteen of you. So you're bound to keep running into each other. It's really a neat way the camp has of making sure you get to know everyone here. That's why they limit the camp to sixteen kids."

We four just grinned and had no questions. First of all we knew we could check with Alissa if we did have questions, and secondly, Karen made it pretty simple.

She gave us our schedules and said that we had an hour to get ready for dinner. "Remember skirts or skorts, and Alissa, you need to get down to the kitchen as quickly as possible." Longtermers were on K. P. every Sunday.

I looked over my schedule and saw that I was on Grounds

and Gardens today. "Great. So what do I do about that chore?" I asked.

"Hey, it's no big deal, 'cause the staff gardener knows you just got here and he probably did it anyway," Alissa said. "After you get dressed for dinner just go out to the greenhouse and introduce yourself and ask him what you'll be doing on Thursday, when it's your day again. You will be okay and Joe will be glad you took the time to stop in at the greenhouse."

"Thanks, Alissa. I'm sure glad you know the ropes around here. I actually have gardened before with my grandma. We've had some fun experiences," I explained to her.

I quickly changed into my skort and shirt, shoved on a pair of sandals and scooted down to the greenhouse to meet Joe. "Hi, Joe, I'm Sam, and I have Grounds and Gardens today for my chore. I know I probably haven't time now to help, but I could run out after dinner to something if you wanted me to."

Joe was an interesting looking man. He was probably about 40 something, wore dirty overalls and had a neat beard. His hands looked callused from his work, and his arms were tanned from being in the sun. He had a ready smile and blue eyes that sparkled when he spoke.

"Sure thing, little Missy. I have to get cleaned up myself for dinner, so how about you stopping in afterwards and I can kind of explain just what we do?" smiled Joe, with crinkles around his eyes, like he knew something special that was just bursting to get out.

"I'll come back then." As I turned to go I saw this huge, monstrous dog. His head had to be at least ten inches wide. He was lying on the floor right in front of the door. "Wow, is that a huge dog or a small pony?" I questioned, jokingly. "I've never seen a dog that big. What kind is he?"

"That's Blodin, and he is a mastiff," answered Joe, with a smile. He is a huge one, for sure, but he's as gentle as a puppy. I'm sure you and he will get along just fine. All the kids just love him. In fact they spoil him rotten, sneaking food down from dinner. Now run along Missy and I'll see you at dinner."

Chapter Five
Dinner and the Staff

I hurried back to the house and found everyone gathering outside the dining room. When we had our tour I had noticed a large table and assumed that all the kids ate at one table. WRONG! That was for the administrators and all the staff. Karen was telling us where our table would be. There were four tables for the campers and their counselors—four round tables with places for five. The dining room looked like a big conference room, or a ballroom with lots of tables.

We all went in and, believe it or not, we were in awe. The Table Trotters were standing behind a chair. Hannah was there at our table. Karen and all the counselors led their group in and we all stood behind a chair. The head table started singing grace. Then they started it again, and each of the counselors and long termers started in as in a round. They sang it through three times, and by then we all knew the words and were joining in. "For food and drink and daily bread we praise thy name oh Lord." When we all finished the echo of the grace lingered in the vast room, and we all pulled out our chairs and sat down.

The Table Trotters immediately went to the serving counter and started carrying over the platters and dishes of food. There was a big pitcher of milk on the table, bread and butter, and the salt and pepper.

All the other food was carried over by the trotters and handed to the counselor. She helped herself and passed it to her left. Hannah's place was to Karen's right, and as the food got passed around it ended up at Hannah's place. When she got done serving, the food was right there for her. She had to make sure there was plenty of everything and had to go back for seconds if they were needed and requested for by Karen. I wasn't sure she'd have time to eat, but she did.

The menu for Sunday night was great. We had sliced roast beef, mashed potatoes, green beans, cottage cheese, Jell-O, bread and chocolate cake for dessert.

No one went away hungry. I was remembering what Joe had said about the kids supplying Blodin with treats from dinner. I wondered if I could smuggle some roast beef out to him later. I wrapped a bit up in my paper napkin, and hoped and prayed that it wouldn't leak through.

Dinner was a great meal. We all talked and got acquainted better. We shared where we were from, how many were in our families. We had to tell one special thing about our town.

I was the only one from Iowa, and while I came from a city, it was more like a small town compared to some of the others. I'm from Marion, which is basically a suburb of Cedar Rapids. We have about 25,000 people in our town, but compared to the others I am from a small town. Anyhow the special thing I told them about Marion was that it was named for Francis Marion, The Swamp Fox of the Revolutionary War.

He lived from 1732-1795 and was a general. He had secret hideouts in the war, and led daring raids against the British by attacking out of the marshes and vanishing back into them. Marion had formed his men into a guerrilla band, because he didn't have enough men to fight the British in open battle.

The soldiers had to provide their own horses and food. They had their swords made from saw blades and had melted pewter plates for their bullets.

I was fascinated by him, because he sounded so cool. Naturally, he was a part of our Marion history, and so I just told about him.

After dinner the Suds kids, one from each table, gathered up the dirty dishes and took them all back to the kitchen where their job was to scrape the dishes, rinse them and fill the dishwashers. There were two big ones, and they held all the dishes. Amazing!

We were all to meet in the recreation room at seven. The Suds kids were to join everyone as soon as they were done. I checked my watch and saw that I had about eleven minutes to hustle down to the greenhouse to see Blodin and Joe, so I took off. I figured that Blodin would be waiting for me if this was a nightly ritual, but he wasn't anywhere in sight. I called for him, but nothing, no woof or yip. Not that a dog that huge would yip, but there was only silence. Joe wasn't there either, but I didn't think that was too strange as he was at dinner, and I guess he was to go to the rec room too. I left the roast beef in Blodin's dish, and went on back, looking around to see if I could see Blodin around anywhere. I didn't see anything that seemed strange to me. Of course I really didn't know the place at all, so how could I suspect anything?

By the time I got back to the rec room everyone was assembled and Karen kind of gave me a questioning look, like "where were you?" I did a shrug kind of thing with my shoulder kind of pointing outside, and she just smiled. So I guess it was no problem since I was back before everything started.

The entertainment was a short movie of Camp Weemo telling us all about its beginning, what its purpose was, and neat pictures of the different activities that we were going to be doing.

The Chief Administrator introduced all the staff, and they each told about their jobs there. After that the teachers told about all the classes. We had a question and answer time which was really informative after we all lost our shyness and started asking some pertinent stuff.

By eight-thirty it was all over, and we all trooped back to our rooms, took showers, got ready for bed. We sat around and talked until the Taps were blown. It was really cool—the notes just floated out all over the camp and whispered away into the darkness. Karen had turned out the lights when Taps started and it was total quiet all through the house and grounds. I was so excited I was sure I would never get to sleep. I had all these thoughts and ideas and plans for tomorrow running through my head. But of course I did get to sleep.

Chapter Six
The Beginning

Reveille pierced the morning stillness with anticipation and eagerness rushing in to cause near pandemonium in our rooms. We all were so eager to get started with our day. This was the first real day for us, and we were beyond ourselves with excitement.

We showered, dressed, and hustled around squaring our beds away, put our towels up to dry, picked up our stuff and went to the dining hall for breakfast. I'm on Suds today, which means that after breakfast and each meal today, I will be in the kitchen doing the dishes for heaven knows how long.

Alissa did assure me saying, "It really doesn't take that long to do the dishes, because it's just rinsing and putting them in the dishwasher. It's not like you have to sweep the whole dining hall or put them away." Somebody else gets to do that, I guess.

Janis was our Table Trotter and she was kept busy keeping us all supplied with French toast, syrup, fruit juice and milk. It was a neat breakfast and we all were certainly filled up. In fact I was so stuffed that I couldn't really finish my last couple of bites. I wondered if old Blodin would like French toast. I put the pieces in a paper napkin and stuck it in my pocket, hoping it wouldn't leak through before I had a chance to give it to him.

Right after the meal and before anyone left, Joe stood up at the head table and said that we should all keep our eyes open for Blodin. "He didn't come back last night, and while that's not unusual for Blodin to sometimes stay out, he is always back for breakfast. But he wasn't back today. So keep your eyes open, please," said Joe.

Now where in the world would a dog go, away from these grounds? If he'd been somewhere on the grounds you would think he'd have gone back to the greenhouse.

While I was on Suds duty with the other campers, we were discussing what classes we were scheduled for right then. I was supposed to go to Brush and Groom and so was Randy. Mike was scheduled for Stable and Tack and Steph was to be going riding. Steph and Mike were both long-termers and they said not to worry about being late for our class. "The first ten or fifteen minutes of each class is spent in going over instructions and the plan for the day. The leaders know that this first class is Suds for someone and they are good about making sure no one misses out on anything," Steph assured me.

I wondered about my treat for Blodin in my pocket, and decided I had better just dispose of it in the garbage. I didn't think it would be a good idea to have it in my pocket when I was trying to brush and groom a horse.

We finished the dishes in record time, it seemed to me, and Randy and I high-tailed it over to the paddock where eight horses were patiently waiting for us. All the others in the class were already sitting down with a clipboard and a couple of sheets of paper. We got ours and started in reading. It was an instruction page for proper grooming, and a check list to keep track of what we were doing.

"Horses kept in a stable have to be groomed daily using a rubber currycomb, a body brush, a hoof pick and the combs for the tail and the mane," Johnny, the instructor, informed us as he was in the process of gathering up all the grooming tools.

He passed them around to us, and all the while he was telling us about their purpose and how to use them properly, he was demonstrating the long, sweeping brush strokes we were to use. "Always go in the direction of the growth of the hair. This helps to give the coat a healthy glow. Brushing also helps to remove dirt and dandruff.

"Special areas like those touched by the saddle and the girth, and the regions right behind the heels and in the hock depression need special brushing. Then give the horse a thorough wiping with a soft cloth following the brushing."

The hoof pick was used to remove any stones or other objects from the feet. "Examine your horse carefully during grooming for scratches, cuts, lumps, or swollen places. If you find any, be sure to inform me immediately," Johnny told us.

The other sheet had a list with a diagram of all the parts of a horse. We were expected to learn where all these parts were and their names of course. The diagram pointed out the poll (top of the head), forelock, forehead, nostril, muzzle, cheek, neck, mane, shoulder, wither, back, loin, hip, ribs, belly and flank which make up the barrel, the croup, tail, buttock, thigh, stifle and gaskin. Then there was the chest, elbow, forearm, knee, shank, fetlock, pastern and the hoof. I was sure glad there was a picture, because I sure hadn't heard of all those parts before. I hoped I could learn all those names.

Johnny said, "In the winter the horses grow thicker coats that are shed in the spring, but they never shed from their mane or tail. There are no nerves in the roots of the hairs so if they need to be thinned the hairs can be pulled out with no pain to the horse."

I knew they used their tails to swish the flies away, and their skin was able to twitch for the same reason. What I didn't know was that they needed to be covered when resting to maintain a temperature of 101 degrees.

With all that information we were told to go up to a horse and begin to brush and groom it. Now, I'm not afraid of horses, in fact I love them, but I really felt unsure about doing all of this. I picked a smaller horse, a Morgan, Johnny had said, and started in. Her name was Suzy, and she was a deep chestnut brown. A real beauty, as far as I was concerned. She seemed rather stocky and bulky, but I figured that was just the way she was supposed to be.

Johnny worked his way around to all of us, helping us, correcting us or showing us the proper method. He was really patient with all of us, as well as with the horses. When he got over to me he said, "Suzy is the newest horse in the camp. She was purchased just this summer, so we're still getting acquainted. She's supposed to have a colt pretty soon. She doesn't get ridden very much, and spends most of her days lately out in the pasture, waiting."

I guess that explained why I thought she was kind of stocky and bulky. I was so excited to think that she might have her colt while we were here this week. That would be really special. My mind ran off in a million tangents just daydreaming about how that might be, how I might play a part, when all of a sudden she let out a whinny. I was quickly brought back to reality when

Johnny reminded me that I was to be brushing her coat the way the hair grew, not against it. So much for daydreams.

A bell clanged and time was up. We were off to our next class. But not me. This was my break time, and since I had already done my chore of Suds for the morning meal I was free to be on my own.

I knew what I was going to do first. I was going to stop at the greenhouse and see if Blodin was back.

Well, I was sure glad to see him, and told him that I had tried to bring a treat, but decided if he wasn't here it would be a mess by the time he might get it. "So, sorry Blodin, but you missed the treat this time." I gave Blodin a hug and told Joe that I'd stop in again, and I'd see him for sure on Thursday to do the Grounds and Gardens chore.

I still had about a half hour of my break time left, so decided that I'd go back to my room and write a letter home. If I knew me, I'd probably only get one letter written the whole week, so I'd better do it today. At least the folks would hear from me before I arrived back home.

Chapter Seven
Stables and Tack

By ten o'clock I was back down at the stables, for the Stables and Tack class. Tess was the instructor here, and she was a delightful person. She was a bubbly gal with a blond ponytail that swished all the time she was talking. She was so full of energy that she had us all enthused about mucking out the stables and getting them all sweet and clean for the horses. Tess said we were to clean out the stables first and then start in on the tack. We tackled the job with gusto. She gave us each a shovel and a pitch fork and assigned us to a stall. The name up above the door said this stall was Geronimo's. Now I hadn't met him personally yet, but I envisioned him to be a big black beautiful horse.

"What's Geronimo like?" I asked.

Tess said, "He is an American Saddle horse with a blaze on

his forehead. He's big and he's a beautiful black horse." So I was partially right. It's kind of nice to have an idea of the horse whose stall you're cleaning—don't you think?

It didn't take all that long to clean out the stall and toss in the fresh hay for bedding. Then Tess gathered us all together in the hay and had us all sit down while she passed out these sheets of paper. More things to learn, I guess. The sheets had lists of all the tack that we needed to know and were going to be using. Not that the list was long—actually it only included the saddles and the bridle as the tack we were to be accountable for. However, there are two kinds of saddles: The English saddle and the Western saddle. Each part of the saddle was identified in the diagram and Tess said that we were going to be tested on the proper names of the parts of each saddle. Nothing like putting the pressure on us right away. That made our anxiety level go up.

So Kathy and I sat down with our lists and diagrams and began going over all the proper names of the different parts of each saddle.

"This can't be so hard," I decided. "They both have a cantle, which is the back edge of the seat, the seat, which you sit on, and the stirrups," I started out.

"Yeah," Kathy agreed, "but from that point on, the labels are different. The saddle horn on the Western saddle is called the pommel on the English saddle."

"Okay. Got that—saddle horn and pommel. What's next, Kathy?"

"The strap that goes around the horse's belly, is a flank strap on the English saddle and the girth on the western saddle."

"Right—flank strap and girth. Now it's my turn. They both have a skirt, which is just a piece of the saddle and is located on the back of the Western saddle, but on the front of the English saddle. Look at this, Kathy. The piece of leather that holds the stirrup is the stirrup leather on the English Saddle and the fender on the Western one. Plus the fender is lots bigger, too."

"And look, Sam," Kathy said, "the Western saddle has lots of string things to hold gear that the English saddle doesn't have at all."

"At least the bridles are the same. They both have the crownpiece, which goes behind the ears, the browband, which is over the forehead, and the throat latch, which is under the neck."

Kathy continued on, "And the cheek piece, goes along the face, and the noseband goes over the nose. Then there is the bit which holds the reins. The bridle is what controls the horse and the rein, when pulled by the rider cause the bit to put pressure on the lower jaw and pulls on the corner of the horse's lips."

We tested each other and then went over to the saddles and practiced on the real thing. I kept getting the string and strap things on the western saddle mixed up, but finally got them straight in my mind. I felt I was ready to be tested.

Tess had us go over to her when we felt we were ready to name all the parts of the saddles. Kathy and I were confident that we knew them okay, so we went. I went first, and wished I had gone second, because I got mixed up on the saddle strings and the hobble strap. I caught it though, so I was okay. The English saddle was a snap though and I whizzed right through it. Kathy did great, too…so we both passed with flying colors.

Kathy said, "The other classes for stables and tack will be practicing how to put the tack on properly, getting the girth straps the right tightness and putting the tack away properly."

"That's right," I agreed. "Remember that Tess said that getting everything in the right place is very important so that when anyone goes out to saddle up a horse, everything for that horse would be in the right place."

I couldn't believe how quickly the classes went. When the bell rang Tess said, "Those of you who have fishing next will have to hightail it right down to the lake." Shoot, I wasn't even sure where the lake was, but Alex said he was going there, and as he was familiar with it we could go there together.

I never did figure out how they set up our schedules, but it did work. Fishing was a blast. The lake had three docks that we could fish from, and the poles, bait, nets, and hooks were right there waiting for us. A couple of the kids in our group had never fished before, and Charlie, our leader, took them over to one dock and got them going. I was sure glad that Grandpa and I had fished before, and I knew what to do.

"This is a catch and release pond," Charlie said, "as we really don't need to supply the meals for the camp. The pond has walleyes, crappies, blue gills, bass and a really large, old catfish. Old Whiskers, is one elusive catfish. The challenge of the week will be to see if anyone can catch Old Whiskers." Of course the seasoned fishermen were sure they could. "Old Whiskers weighs at least thirty pounds, so," we were warned, "if you're going to try to snag Old Whiskers, you'd better have some heavy line on the pole you use."

Charlie said there was a contest each week to see who caught the most, the longest, and the heaviest fish. So we each had this chart and we were expected to record the stats for our fish. Each dock had a scale and a ruler to measure and weigh the fish. We had to date each entry so we would have an accurate record. Two or three of us fished from the same dock, and it was a fun time.

That first day I had three or four snags. There must have been a tree or branches under the water, and I managed to find them quite often. I figured out how to pull my line taut, let it snap and pull, and finally I got the hang of getting out of snags without losing too many of my hooks.

I had only four days to catch Old Whiskers, because on Wednesday I had K. P. during fishing. The contest was only for four days anyway so each of the K. P. kids had equal chance.

One day would be devoted to tying lures. I was excited about that because, my brother, Cody, was in Scouts and they were going to learn how to tie lures. For once I was going to do something neat before he did it in Scouts.

Our grandpa had been a Scout Leader a long time ago, when he and Grandma lived in a small town where all their kids were born. Grandma taught school and Grandpa had a meat processing plant there. Grandpa and one of his friends were the Scout leaders, and it was fun to hear all the stories Grandpa told about their camping trips and their cookouts. Anyhow, Cody was really looking forward to doing all kinds of fun things as a Scout.

Chapter Eight
Camping Skills

I was sure that this class would be something I had at least a little knowledge in because our family had gone camping all our lives. We have a cottage at Delhi, but we didn't always have a cottage. I can remember tenting on our property—because that's all we had—property. Dad and Mom had bought a cottage upstream earlier, but the water was so shallow that we sunk in the mud whenever we waded out into it. Then you should have seen our toes—well, our toenails, I mean. They were yellow, a dull yellow from the mud, like a bullhead yellow.

Cody and I did learn to water ski there, and we had fun, but when Dad had a chance to buy a couple of lots farther down stream he did, and that's the property I'm talking about.

We tented the first summer on that property and let me tell you that a tent with five people can get rather crowded, even if three of us were kids. Especially on rainy weekends. Shannon wasn't born yet, then, so she never has had to tent.

The second summer at Delhi, Mom and Dad decided we needed a trailer. It was something else again. The whole trailer bit is a story in its own. Mom, Cody, Cameron and I were the ones to go get it. It was the fall before Shannon was born, so I was ten, Cody was seven and Cameron was four. It was supposed to be "no sweat" to quote Dad. Ha! It was a Friday afternoon, and we had been let out of school early because of the heat. Mom had to take us along, which I suppose was a blessing in disguise. Anyhow we got to Delhi and up on the road where they were supposed to take the trailer down to our spot.

In the first place they weren't there, so we had to wait. Then when the guy got there with the trailer he got out and looked at the hill he was supposed to drive down and said, "Sorry, Lady. This is as far as I can go. No way can I drive this rig down THAT hill. I'll just park it over there along the side of the road and you'll have to get somebody else to take it down."

"Hey, wait a minute, Mister. What am I supposed to do? It's already after one, and I don't know anyone around here to get to take it down. Are you sure you can't do it? Did you check out the whole road? It's not that bad. We drive up and down this hill all the time with no problem," Mom countered.

"That may be, but no way can I maneuver this hill and those

curves with this much of a load with no counter weight," stated the driver.

And with that he climbed back in his truck, parked the trailer on the edge of the road, backed out and drove off. Mom was standing there with her mouth open and we kids weren't sure what was going to happen next. Well, of all things, it started to rain. I mean not just little sprinkles, either, but those huge drops. I think Mom wanted to join in herself, because she sure looked like she was about to cry.

"Hey, Mom, come on back in the car. You're getting all wet", I coaxed her, big problem solver that I was. She got in, and then the boys decided they were hungry.

This was all just supposed to take a little bit to show the guy where the trailer was to be and then we were going to get hamburgers and fries in town.

"You're right, kids. We'll go get something to eat while it's raining, and maybe I can figure something out about what to do with this *thing*," agreed Mom.

That trailer was a weird thing. It was maybe 35 feet long and was an eight foot wide monster. Actually, believe it or not this trailer was a two story job, painted pink on top and blue on the bottom. Even I could understand not wanting to pull that thing down a steep hill with the lake at the bottom.

We took off for town, probably a couple of miles down the road, and found a local greasy spoon joint. Actually, their hamburgers were the best I'd had in a long time. Maybe because we were hungry, but whatever it was, they were good.

Mom asked the waitress, "Do you know anyone around who moves trailers down to the lake property?"

"Sure, my brothers do it all the time. They have these two big tractors and they hook one on the front and one on the back and take them down slicker than a whistle."

"So where can I reach your brothers?" asked Mom.

"Well, they should be in the fields picking corn, but since it started to rain they'll probably be in here anytime for lunch," was her answer.

Mom thanked her, and said we'd stay awhile, but if they didn't come in we'd just get their phone number and Dad could call them tonight. That is actually what we did. We ate, and got their number and went home. I couldn't believe our luck—good and bad—and we still got home before Dad got home from work.

That was the beginning of camping life for us at Delhi. The trailer had two bedrooms upstairs for us, and it had a big bathroom and a galley type kitchen and a living room area on the main level. Dad soon built on a porch and screened it in for a living room, and the kitchen was expanded into the old living room. We put a big table in there and had a nice dining room. Dad also built bunk beds for the boys out on the porch which gave me a room to myself for a while.

The stove wasn't very usable, so we cooked all our meals over a fire, and since we didn't have hot water, we heated it in kettles over the fire, too. We washed the dishes at the picnic table.

Actually our camping experiences taught us how to survive, how to build a good campfire, and our family has some neat memories of sitting around the fire before bedtime playing charades.

I still have plenty to learn about Camping Skills in this class. That first day we got a schedule for the week, and it included fire building, but three different types. We were also going to build a latrine, and cook over the campfire. The menus were to include one meal dishes, desserts, cooking chicken on a spit, and roasting potatoes and carrots over the fire. I think we will have a fun time in this class.

Chapter Nine
Riding

I woke up with the knowledge that it was Tuesday, and this was my day to be Table-trotter. That meant that I would be the last one to get my food, plus I had to be sure that whenever a tray or bowl was empty I would have to go get some more.

I hurried through my morning routine and got down to the dining hall in record time. I had to check out the food to see just what I was going to have to trot to our table. The breakfast menu was a simple one today, just cold cereal, toast, juice and milk. That should be a piece of cake.

I was eager to get back to my riding class today. Yesterday was a typical first day for the class. We got acquainted, told what we knew about riding, if we had in fact ever ridden before, etc., etc., etc. I couldn't believe that anyone would be here at this camp if they hadn't ridden before, but I guess there's a first time for everyone. In our riding group it was Leslie who hadn't ever ridden a horse before. She was from Florida and just never had the opportunity to ride, I guess.

Anyhow, we had a good group, and Hank, our instructor, seemed really pleased that so many of us did have some riding skills. That's why I was so excited about today. Hank had said that the north timber had neat riding trails, and the meadow was an excellent place to canter and gallop. He had said that there was no worry about getting lost as the whole complex was fenced in.

"Mornin' kids. Ready to ride?" Hank asked. He had taken a quick roll call and checked us all in while we were arriving. "You kids seem pretty confident around the horses, so you're going to be on your own today. You have forty-five minutes so check your watches and ride out for half that time and then return.

You need to be here in time to put the horses back and before the next group comes. The Grooming group will brush them down and take care of them, but you'll need to return the tack to the tack room.

I expect you to be responsible riders and conscientious about what you're doing. You'll ride in pairs, so check the schedule to see who you are with today. We'll trade off every day, so you'll have different partners. I'll ride with Leslie and

Randy today, and each day I'll ride with two others. Any questions?"

I couldn't believe that on just the second day we were able to be on our own, so to speak. I glanced at the roster and nearly fainted when I saw I was paired up with Josh. He was one of the guys that had been on my flight here and was an awesome guy. He had real dark hair, and deep brown eyes. His skin was more olive than tanned, and he looked like a real cowboy. He had been in the Stable and Tack class with me and was partnered with Kenny for testing. He didn't even notice me, I'm sure. But I sure noticed him. Now I was going to get to go riding with him, over the meadows and through the woods, and who knew where else? I remember when we were all introducing ourselves he said his dad was English and his mom Italian. Her name was Salvianti…or something like that. Whatever they were they had a neat looking son.

We went to the stables and got our horses. We got the tack from the tack room and saddled up. I was riding Brindle today. She seemed to be a decent horse while I was getting her gear on her. I noticed that Josh had Geronimo. Just that name seemed exciting. I had cleaned out his stall and Tess, the instructor, had said he was an American saddle horse. He was a beautiful black with a blaze on his forehead. He was a lot bigger than Brindle, as she was a Morgan, like Suzy. Suzy was the horse I'd groomed that first day. She was the newest horse at the camp and also expecting a colt.

I noticed that Suzy wasn't there in her stall. "Hey, Hank. I don't see Suzy in here, and I didn't notice her outside either. Where is she?"

"She and a couple of the others are out in the north pasture. We let the horses be on their own periodically so they get used to our land. Suzy is with a couple of the older mares and they will teach her what she needs to learn about Camp Weemo. They'll show her the water holes and streams, good pasture ground and generally help her to be better oriented about this place. Kind of how your counselors helped you get acquainted around here. It works for the new horses, too."

"Come on, Sam, time's slipping by. Hurry up and get mounted so we can be off," Josh said, sitting proudly on Geronimo. He looked like he really belonged on a horse and was so at ease. I wasn't so sure I'd be quite as confident. Oh, I've ridden enough, but somehow Josh just looked right.

"I'm coming, I'm coming," I called back.

We took off across the pasture area and settled into an easy trot. Brindle responded well to my gentle pulls on the bridle. She was well trained and I soon felt very much at ease.

At first Josh and I didn't say much. We just rode and enjoyed the scenery and the beautiful morning. In the distance we could see a stream and could see that it meandered down into a gorge-like area. We decided to ride over by the stream and check it out.

"I wonder if there are any caves along there?" Josh pointed out. "Remember that first night at dinner when we all had to introduce ourselves and tell something about our state? You told about Marion Francis, the Swamp Fox."

"My gosh, you can remember that! How'd you remember it was me? There were so many of us all telling stuff. I can't believe you remember about that."

"Yeah, well, I like history and that kind of stuff. You made it sound pretty exciting. We have a Marion, Wisconsin, too, but I haven't the slightest idea if it was named for him or not. Marion is just a small town that we go through on our way to Blue Mounds where we have our famous Cave of the Mounds."

"That's right. I remember you telling about the caves and all the stalactites and stalagmites, and the streams and passages and rooms in the caves. It was great what you said about the caves, almost like a report."

"That's because I did do a report on it at school, right before the end of the year. I had done a lot of research on caves and spelunking for the report and I really got into it. I'd love to find one here and go exploring."

"Spel…what?"

"Spelunking. That's exploring through caves as a hobby. A

person who does spelunking is a spelunker," Josh said. "Hey, check the time, Sam. We've got to get back. Maybe on one of our free times we could ride out here and check out the caves. I'm sure there will be some over on the other side of the stream."

The ride back to camp gave us some time to get to know each other. Always before we were just in classes together and really didn't have time to get to know each other.

"I live right outside of Rhilelander. Actually we have a deer reserve and have hundreds of deer protected on our land. I have two brothers and two sisters. I'm in the middle—the youngest of the boys and older than my sisters."

I had a chance to tell about my brothers and sister, too, and before we knew it we were back at camp.

"Check out your schedule, Sam, and let's see if we have any free time coming up."

We took our horses back to the paddock where we took off the saddle, bridle and blanket and took them back to the tack room.

I grabbed my schedule out of my pocket and Josh had his out, too, looking it over. "I'm free for a couple of hours on Thursday afternoon. Would that work for you?" Josh asked.

"That's great for me, too. Do you suppose we could get horses for the ride out? Let's ask Hank," I suggested.

We explained to Hank that on our ride we saw what

appeared to be a cave across the stream to the north. We told him we had some free time for swimming and tennis on Thursday and wanted permission to ride back to the cave instead.

"I can't see any problem with that, as long as it's your free time and you let your counselors know where you'll be. Be sure to take flashlights and jackets. It's only 52 degrees in caves all the time. Since your free time is from two to four you'll have plenty of time to get back and get cleaned up for the evening meal. Sounds good. Be sure you let me know what you discover. If you want, you two can take Brindle and Geronimo again, since you're familiar with them. They're really reliable horses, too," Hank said. "You'd better hustle on to your next session, or you'll be late."

Chapter Ten
Chuck Wagons and Hayrides

I woke up early because this was my day for K. P. We had to be down at the kitchen an hour before the meal was to be served. In the morning we went over the menu for the day and got our assignments of what we were going to have to be responsible for. Janis had already been on K. P. yesterday and clued me in last night. I jumped up, got dressed, made my bed and stopped by the bathroom to quickly wash my face and brush my teeth.

Today's menus were easy enough. For breakfast we'll have to fix scrambled eggs, bacon, toast and juice. Lunch is going to be soup and sandwiches, with choices of potato or chicken noodle for the soups, and ham and cheese, tuna or chicken salad, and of course the old standby, to rescue the picky eaters, peanut butter sandwiches. Tonight was a special night. We were going to have a chuck wagon meal and hayrack ride. The menu then will be sloppy Joes, baked beans, veggies, chips and a cherry cobbler dessert that was going to be cooked over the fire in a Dutch oven type of kettle. It all sounded good to me. Of course, why wouldn't it? I'm starving right now after talking about all that food.

I was assigned the toast for breakfast, the chicken salad sandwiches for lunch and the sloppy Joes for the chuck wagon meal. I could handle all that with no problems.

Breakfast went great and in no time at all I was sitting down with our group and starting out on our third whole day of camp.

I looked around the dining hall and spotted Josh at his table. Our eyes met across the room and he raised his eyebrows and winked at me. I couldn't believe he did that, but I grinned back at him, and I know my face got beet red because Janis looked over at me and asked me if I was okay. "Sure, I just swallowed something the wrong way," I said, coughing a bit. "I'm fine. No problem." I wasn't about to tell her right there that Josh had just winked at me. I snuck a look back at him but he was busy talking to Kenny and didn't even look my way again. I'm sure he could tell that I blushed right down to the roots of my hair. Great.

Sessions went great today, and today was my day for canoeing. When Josh and I were comparing our schedules we discovered that we had Canoeing at the same time on Wednesday. I was looking forward to having another class with him.

Again this was something that I knew how to do. We had a canoe at the lake, so just last summer Dad taught me how to paddle and steer. Cody, my nine year old brother, begged to be able to go out, too, but Dad said not until he could swim better. I've passed all my swimming classes except for life saving, and I have to be fifteen to qualify for that, I think. Whatever, I just know that I'm not old enough yet. But I am a good swimmer and the folks trust me in the water. At the lake though we always have to wear life jackets while in the water, because it is so deep right off the end of our dock. So I do, not that I like it very much, but since I have to I do.

Angela was the instructor for Canoeing. This was our second day of Canoeing as it alternated with fishing. We were scheduled for four sessions of each. "Your first day of Canoeing was either yesterday or Monday, depending on your schedules. I checked you out as to your abilities in canoeing, and determined your skill level. Now we can use that information today."

That was how she determined what our route was going to be today. The Canoeing class and the fishing class both had different kids on different days because of the K. P. schedules, and other scheduling concerns. That's why Josh wasn't in my class on Monday and was today, I guess.

When we got to the lake we put on our life jackets and sat down on the dock. "Okay, campers. Today you'll get to prove how good you are. You're going on a treasure hunt and will have ten items that you have to locate and bring back to the dock."

Angela had a lake map all ready for the four groups. The kids who were level two had maps that the route kept them in sight of the dock. The level one kids were able to go beyond the trees on the island in the lake and come back around. We had to follow clues to paddle to a certain area or land mark, find our 'treasure' and go on to the next clue. It sounded like fun and a good way to practice our canoeing skills. We were going to have to canoe into shore, get out, find the 'treasure' and the next clue and get back in the canoe without tipping it over.

Needless to say we had a ball. Hannah and I were in one canoe and Josh and Alex were in another. Beth and Janis were in the third one and Randy and Eddie were in the fourth. Beth and Janis and Randy and Eddie were new at canoeing and had to stay in sight of the dock, but the other four of us could go beyond the island.

Obviously the treasures were planted on the shore, as they were not native stuff. We had to find a small box, an acorn, a feather, a bobber, a toy spyglass, a seashell, a rubber duck, a plastic fish, a Snicker candy bar, and a can of pop. Our instructions gave us a clue as to where to find the next one and then when we got to the candy bar and pop we were instructed to wait until we got back to the dock to eat them.

On the far side of the island as I was paddling up in the front, I accidentally splashed Josh and Alex as they were approaching us. I swear I didn't mean to get them wet, but I sure did.

"Hey, you jerks. You got us all wet. Boy you'd better look out!"

"Sorry. I really am. A little water won't hurt you. You'll be dry before we get back. Wait a minute, what are you doing? Come on you guys. It was an accident…"

Whhooosh. Wow, they both scooped their paddles across the water and drenched Hannah and me. We were soaked and not just a few sprinkles either, like I had done to them.

We were dripping. The water was running into my eyes, and my hair went perfectly straight. I couldn't believe they did this. Plus they were laughing. *Laughing* like it was a huge joke.

I turned around to check out Hannah and she looked as bad as I felt, but she had this quirky little smile on her face and when she saw me looking like a drowned rat, she burst into gales of laughter. Now she was laughing and before I knew it, she grabbed her paddle, and shoved our canoe away from theirs.

Alex had just stood up, a 'no,no' in a canoe, at the exact

instant that Hannah pushed off from it, and before anyone could say anything the whole thing tipped over. Josh, Alex and the canoe were all under water.

Now I really got concerned, because I've always been one who follows the rules and tries to do what is right. You know the type. Well, that was me. Now Josh and Alex were soaked and having a ball in the lake. Hannah looked like she was ready to jump in with them and join in on the fun and I was sitting there having a conniption fit. My gosh, what was Angela going to do to us? I couldn't even imagine. I suppose it was only a couple of minutes before we all came to our senses and the boys righted their canoe and while Hannah and I held onto the sides, they got back in. I've never righted a canoe in my life. Dad and I never got that far in our instructions, and I don't know how they managed, but they did.

By now we were all soaked, and we, at least Hannah and I, still had to find three more of the 'treasures' before we were done. Josh said that he and Alex only had two more to go. We quick compared lists and clues and figured out very quickly where we had to go.

I'll never forget that day. The neatest part was that no one got mad, and when we finally made it back to the dock we were all fairly dry—especially the guys. Angela had a few words for us, but we could tell that she really wasn't mad at us, and actually pleased that the boys had been able to right the canoe. She said that was our next lesson, anyway.

Finally the preparations for the chuck wagon meal were done and all the rest of the campers were trooping over the meadow to where we were having our meal. There were a couple of big tables set up and at the end of each one was a big tub filled with pop, orange drink and milk. This was one meal that we didn't have to be dressed up and we could sit anywhere we wanted.

Josh came over to me and asked, "Where are you sitting, Sam?" like it was the most natural thing in the world. I kind of stuttered and just pointed to a spot at the nearest table. "Fine, how about if I join you, if you don't mind."

"I don't mind at all. That'd be great," I said, after I finally found my voice. This was too good to be true. I mean, Josh is one of the neatest guys here this week and he wanted to sit with me.

"Is it okay if Alex and Hannah sit there, too?"

"Great, no problem." I was in seventh heaven. Anybody who wanted could sit anywhere they wished, I could care less. I had a feeling that I wouldn't even know who was there, as long as Josh and I were sitting beside each other. Things were looking better and better.

The food was great, even if I do say so myself, since I was on K. P. I don't know if it was because of our canoeing that I was so starved, or just eating outdoors, but I can't believe how much I ate. I hope I didn't eat as much as Josh, because he was really packing it in. I was hardly aware of eating since we were sitting together.

I know we kept up a running conversation about a ton of things, but afterwards when Janis and I were talking about it, I couldn't remember a word I had said.

Janis said, "You can't remember anything 'cause you have a crush on Josh."

I pooh-poohed the idea, but I think I probably do, although I wasn't about to admit it. He sure is one special guy.

After the meal the Camp Director got up and said that there were two hay wagons ready for a trail ride and that once everything was cleaned up from the meal we'd be ready to go. You can't imagine how quickly everything got picked up, thrown away or packed away in the van and we were ready to go.

"Come on, Sam, let's get started with the clean up." Josh worked right along beside me the whole time, and when it was time to get on the hayrack he grabbed my hand and helped me up on the nearest one. "Let's go."

We got settled in the hay and before long the horses started plodding along. I glanced towards the front to see which horses were hitched up to our hayrack and noticed they were two of the older ones. I guess a slow paced walk was great for them.

Josh kept hold of my hand for a long time after we got settled on the hayrack and it felt pretty good to hold hands with a guy. I haven't had any real boyfriends. Oh, I have *boy* friends, but that's not what I mean. Maybe I did have a crush on him. He sure seemed to like holding my hand. Maybe he liked me, too.

We all started singing and I couldn't believe the songs we were singing. They were all the ones we had sung as little kids. We sang "Row, Row, Row, Your Boat", as a round, and "Frere Jacques," too. We also sang "Down By the Station", "Old Mac Donald", "B-I-N-G-O", and a bunch of others. I can't even remember them all. We even sang "Ninety-nine Bottles of Beer on the Wall". I figured the counselors would make us quit that one, but we went through the whole thing.

By that time we were just about back to camp. The horses took us all the way back to the stables, so we really didn't have that far to go back to the house.

Josh held my hand all the way back to the house and we talked about tomorrow and going to see the caves. He said, "Don't forget to bring a flashlight and a sweatshirt and a jacket."

When we got outside the house he stopped and we turned to look at each other. "I really had a great time tonight, Sam. You're a fun person to be with." Then he leaned over a bit and gave me a little kiss on my cheek.

You could have knocked me over with a feather. That was the last thing I expected Josh to do. "Thanks, Josh. I had fun, too. It will be a really special memory of camp."

Then we just turned and went in and up to our own areas. Before we parted Josh said, "See you tomorrow, Sam. Sleep tight."

Chapter Eleven
The Caves

Finally it was Thursday and Josh and I were going to go to the caves. I had talked with Karen about it, and she gave me permission to go. I was sure Josh had talked with Greg, his counselor, too, since we were talking about it yesterday.

I had the Garden and Grounds duty today and went down to check with Joe about what I was supposed to do today. I had brought a few pieces of pancakes for Blodin, but once again when I got there he was gone. He must be an independent thing, because he was always off doing his own thing it seemed. Joe wasn't there either—which was strange.

When I got there I saw that Joe had left me a list of what I had to do. I had the trimming to do around the edge of the walks. I worked steady on that for thirty minutes and thought I was going to die. The edger thing I had to use got so heavy.

I couldn't believe that Janis or Alissa could have kept up that pace. Not as little as they are. I think I got put on that job because I was the giant.

Finally the time was up, and Joe came back. "Wow, Missy. You really did a fine job. I didn't expect you to keep at it this long. I would have been back sooner, but I got detained. I should have been here while you were working. Sorry about that."

"That's okay," I said, but hardly feeling that it was okay. I was beat, but the fact that I really did more than Joe expected me to do did make me feel better about the whole deal. "Did Blodin ever get back?" I asked.

"Yes, the old scalawag. I swear he's been going farther and farther every night. I'd like to follow him to see just where he is off to when he takes off like that. In fact that's where I was. I was checking with Hank to see if Blodin was with the horses out in the north meadow. Hank had mentioned once that Blodin seemed to hang around the stables quite a bit. But Hank said that he hadn't seen Blodin around there today."

"It's such great weather he probably is enjoying his freedom and had a great run. He sure can't get into trouble here at the Camp. Everything is in such great shape." I hated to run off, but when I checked my watch I saw that it was already nearly two. I still had to get back and pick up my flashlight and jacket and sweatshirt. I already had on my jeans and heavy shoes from gardening, so I was set for that. "Take care, Joe. I've enjoyed working with you this week, and I really did learn how to edge the lawn. My folks will be pleased about that, especially my dad, since he usually does that at home. See you later."

I took off and ran all the way back to get my stuff and five minutes later I was down at the stable. Josh was already there and had both Geronimo and Brindle ready to go. "Thanks, Josh. I couldn't get away from Joe today. I had to edge the walks up by the front of the house. Golly, what a chore that was. I was about beat, but I kept thinking about the cave and that kept me going."

"I was hoping you hadn't changed your mind."

"No way. I've been looking forward to this for forever, it seems. Was it only two days ago that we found them?"

Josh put his arm around me and gave me a little squeeze and said, "Hop on up and let's go. I'll beat you to the trees." With that he sharply turned Geronimo and cantered off across the meadow. I followed on Brindle keeping up with them.

The ride to the trees was exhilarating. I had never felt so alive before in my whole life. The wind whipped my auburn hair back away from my face and I felt as if there was no one else in the whole world but Josh and me. I was looking forward to exploring the caves. I was with a special friend and I was riding a great horse. I felt like I could go on like this forever.

We slowed the horses down to a walk and let them catch

their breath. We had stopped by the stream so we let the horses get their fill. I had brought along a water bottle at the last minute and was glad I had. I shared it with Josh and it was sweet and cold. I wondered if we could fill it up with the stream water, but didn't suggest it.

We were right across from where we had seen the cave on Tuesday. The horses didn't even balk at all when we urged them into the water. It was a shallow stream and we could see the chubs and fingerlings swimming in it. "Hey, this is a trout stream. I wonder if there are bears in Kentucky. What if one is using that cave we're planning on exploring? I mean, do we have to worry about bears or anything else that might be in the cave?"

"No. I don't think so any way. If we were going to have a problem coming here to explore I think Hank would have said something, or Greg. Did Karen say anything about that to you?"

"No, she just said to be sure to get back in time to get dressed for dinner."

Once we reached the cave we tethered our horses outside of it to a small tree. There was plenty of grass for them to eat, and shade under the tree.

Josh put his sweatshirt on and tied his jacket around his waist. I followed his example, remembering about the 52 degree temperature that Hank had mentioned.

"I'll go in first and you follow. We won't need our flashlights right away, but if it takes a turn then we will."

"I can feel the difference in temperature already. I think we'll be glad that we have our jackets, too. Can you see anything yet? I can tell that the floor is damp. I have to be careful so I don't slip. Can you see anything yet?" I rattled on.

"Come up here beside me, Sam. We've just come into a large room-like area. It's beautiful."

I stood beside Josh and saw what he meant. The cave had opened up and we could see where the water had seeped through the cracks. The limestone was dissolved and we were standing in a large room. We flashed our lights all around and the wet rocks gave off brilliant colors. It was a beautiful sight. Over to the side there were great icicle-shaped formations hanging from the ceiling. "Those are the stalactites. They are the ones that form from the water dripping down. The stalagmites are the formations that build up from the floor. When they meet, like those over there," Josh indicated with his beam of light, "then columns are formed. Because the dissolved limestone is carried in the water, the columns are actually stone that has built up. Where the stone dissolved more slowly is where we'll find just passages, rather than large rooms, like this one. Do you want to go in farther to see if we can find some passages and maybe an underground lake?"

I shivered with the excitement as well as the chill of the cave, and said, "Let's go. Lead on Sir Josh and I will follow thee."

We went further along and came to a Y in the passage. Josh aimed his light both ways and could see nothing ahead. The light just didn't penetrate very far at all. It was cold and damp and now eerie as well. We knew that bats might be in there, but so far hadn't startled any from their sleep. "You know that not much lives in caves. Oh, bears and snakes might use them to hibernate in, and other animals might be in them too, in the winter, but right now I doubt that there is anything in here. If we should find a lake in here, maybe it would have some fish. But because there is no light in here they would have white skins and their eyes would be useless," Josh informed me, like a tour guide might.

"Is this passage getting smaller, or is it just me?" I asked.

"You're right. It's getting smaller and narrower. Are you game to follow it along farther to see how far we can go?"

"Sure, I think."

We crept along and all the time we had to keep bending over lower and lower the farther we went into the passage. Finally Josh started to get down on his knees to crawl through a very small opening. "I don't know if you should go through there. What if you'd get stuck?" I said.

"I'll be fine. You wait right there and I'll see how far it will go. If it opens up I'll call for you to come. Otherwise I'll just back out to where you'll be waiting for me. You will wait, won't you?"

"Of course I will silly. Where would I go? I'm not even sure if I know the right way to go back, anyhow. It's already a quarter of three. It took us twenty minutes to ride here on the horses, and we've been in the cave for twenty-five minutes.

"You be back here or call for me in ten minutes. That should give us enough time to get back out and return to camp in time. Now remember, don't leave me here any longer than ten minutes. I'm not sure I can stand this claustrophobia too long. It's so tight and closed up in here."

"You'll be fine, Sam, I promise. I'll be back in ten minutes, no longer, or I'll call for you to come on through and join me. I'll see you soon. You going to be okay?"

"I'll be here, waiting."

Did you ever think about how long ten minutes is? Thank Heavens I had my watch. You only have to count to six hundred and that is ten minutes, but I kept forgetting what number I was on. I was positive I could hear bats moving around behind me, and I was sure that when I did get outside again I would be blinded by the sun. I couldn't hear Josh moving around and I was afraid he'd fallen into a hole or got stuck or disappeared altogether. I kept my light on my watch, but the hands barely moved while I watched. I decided not to watch. The time still didn't pass fast enough to suit me.

Faintly I heard my name. "Sam,—Sam—can you hear me?"
"Yes," I hollered.

"Come on, Sam. It's safe. Come on and just keep going straight. It opens up after a bit and you'll be able to stand up. Come on."

Thank Heavens, I could go forward. I crept along, the light pointed to the ground so I could see where I was creeping. I kept hearing Josh talking and encouraging me along. I was sure I had waited the full ten minutes, but obviously it wasn't that long, because shortly I was able to stand up and I could see Josh.

The sun was streaming in behind him and I could see that he was standing in a beautiful large room again. It was much like the one we had started in. In fact I wondered if we had been walking in a circle and had just completed it. "Are we back where we started? Is this that first room we were in?" I said.

"No, this is another entrance. We're on the other side of the hill. I looked out of this entrance, and our horses aren't here. I figured we are a good half hour from the horses. How are you at jogging across this rough terrain?"

"I'm with you all the way, Josh. Let's go. I don't guarantee that I can jog all the way, but I'll try to keep up. I don't usually get side aches, but if I do you just keep on going. I'll catch up."

I sounded brave, but to be honest I was scared stiff. I never was a track person, and sprints were more my style. Long distance runs or cross country stuff didn't interest me at all. Maybe I'll feel differently after this is all over, but I doubt it.

We took off and sure enough it wasn't long before I could feel that stitch in my side. I slowed down, and when Josh turned to look at me I just waved him on. I had to rest a minute. That's all it took, just a brief rest and I was on my way again. I could see Josh still running ahead of me. My watch let me know that it was already ten after three. We still couldn't see the horses—at least I couldn't see them from where I was. Now I couldn't even see Josh. He must have come to a curve and was just out of my sight. I hoped.

All of a sudden I saw them…Josh and the horses. He had made it all the way back and was coming back for me. What a wonderful sight that was to see them. I just sat down where I was and waited. I don't think I could have taken another step if my life had depended on it.

"Way to go, Josh. You're my hero…my knight in shining armor. You've rescued the maiden in distress."

"Well, my Princess, how about mounting this fine steed and riding away with me into the night? Or at least back to camp so we can be there in time for dinner. I'm table trotter tonight you know and there are four others who will be counting on me to serve them."

Chapter Twelve
The Final Days

Friday night was here and tonight was the final campfire. We had gathered each night outside around the campfire to talk about the day, to sing camp songs, to do skits, to just have a final wind down each night before Taps. It was always a special time for me. I loved the peacefulness of the fire, the glowing embers and the woodsy smell.

Of all the things I had done at camp, this time every night reminded me most of home. Not that I was homesick. I wasn't. I had so much to do each day and had met so many new friends. But the campfire reminded me of when our family went camping. We always sat around the fire at night, too. We usually played charades using nursery rhymes as our topics. The boys were pretty good at them and they and Dad came up with some pretty hilarious actions to give us clues. Mom and I weren't too bad ourselves and it wouldn't be long before Shannon would be joining in.

This night was different, though, because it was the end. All the awards and recognitions had been given out. Everyone got something. The fishing awards were passed out and, lo and behold, I had caught the most fish. No one caught "Old Whiskers" this week, but the last time I had been fishing I caught a glimpse of him swimming by. He was old and huge and I swear he had a twinkle in his eye.

I had a great week, and I knew I'd continue to write to Janis and Hannah. We had become great friends. I felt sad to think of leaving all this behind.

The horses had been great and I knew I would never forget Josh. He was one special guy and we had a terrific friendship started. It was going to be hard to say goodbye to him.

Just as I was starting to head back to the house I felt a hand on my shoulder. I looked back and there was Josh, catching up with me.

"Wait up, Sam. Can we go walk a bit? Do you have to get right back?"

"Let's walk. I'd like that." Already I could feel tears starting to trickle down my cheeks. Thank heavens it was dark and he wouldn't be able to see them.

Josh grabbed my hand and started to turn toward the meadow. "We've had a great time this week, Sam. I'm glad we were able to have so much fun together. At least we'll be on the same flight to Chicago. Then my folks will be picking me up there. How about you? Will your folks be there or what?"

"I will get a flight out of Chicago for Cedar Rapids. It's only about a half hour flight, but I have to wait at O'Hare for an hour to make the connection."

"I'll wait with you, Sam. That way you can meet my folks. I'd like to have them meet you. I've never met a girl like you who is so willing to give anything a shot. You're pretty special, you know."

"That'd be great if your folks don't mind waiting until my flight gets in. I thought I'd just read or something, but I hated the thought of being there all by myself. I managed okay on the flight to camp, because there was no layover. I just went from one plane to the other and had no problems."

Just then Blodin appeared out of the dark. He rushed up to us and nudged us with his mammoth head. "What is it, Blodin? What do you want?" I asked as I knelt down beside the huge dog. He struggled to free himself from my grasp and turned and started off in the direction of the timber. He went a few paces ahead of us and stopped and looked back at us. He whined a bit and started off again. Once again he stopped and looked back at us.

"I think he wants us to follow him," Josh said. "Let's see what's bothering him."

"You know that Blodin had been running at nights. Joe was telling me that he has no idea where he goes. He just shows up later in the morning. Maybe this is where he's been."

We took off running behind Blodin and came to a halt when we saw Suzy lying on her side in the timber. Thank heavens for the moon and the light it gave to the timber. Josh got down and ran his hands over her side. She whinnied and put her head back down. "I think she's ready to foal, Sam. Can you go back and get Hank? I think he'd be the best one. Blodin, go back with Sam," Josh ordered.

I couldn't respond. I just took off with Blodin at my heels. I ran as if my life depended on it. Actually it was Suzy's life, and her foal's who depended on me. No stitch in my side this time. This was the sprint that I'm able to do.

I ran hard and fast and burst through the door of the staffroom. Hank was first to grab me and ask me what was wrong. "Suzy—it's Suzy. She's in the timber ready to foal. Josh is with her. Hurry!"

Hank grabbed his boots and put them on in a run and together we ran back to the timber. Blodin kept right up with us as we ran.

Suzy was still down and Josh was kneeling beside her, softly crooning and making comforting sounds. Hank took over and Josh and I stood back. Evidently because this was Suzy's first colt she was having problems. Hank seemed well aware of the problem. He got Suzy situated and before we knew what had happened a fine little stallion was trying to stand on wobbly legs that looked like toothpicks to me.

Suzy struggled to her legs, nuzzled her colt and gave a whinny of thanks to all of us.

Hank knelt down, picked up the little colt and started back to the stable. Suzy followed and then came Josh, Blodin and me. We made a strange parade back to camp in the middle of the night. Taps were just starting to float out over the night air as we reached camp.

Josh held my hand for a long time and then we turned and gave each other a big hug. Josh kissed me, turned and walked back to the stable. I walked up the flight of stairs filled with wonder at all that had happened that night.

Karen looked up as I walked in and noted the look of awe on my face. The girls all crowded around, all talking at once.

"Where were you?"

"Why weren't you here for Taps?"

"Where'd you go anyway?"

"Were you alone?"

Lights were supposed to be out, but Karen knew that I would have a good reason for not being there. So we all sat on our beds and I told the story about the new colt, but left out the fact that Josh kissed me and was my special friend. That was too new for me to share.

It was forever before we all settled down and Karen made us call it a night and go to bed.

Saturday morning came and with it the hustle and bustle of getting ready for the shuttle to take all of us to Lexington to catch our flights.

Josh and I sat together on the shuttle and talked quietly of what was coming up in our lives. We exchanged our e-mail addresses so we could keep on *talking* to each other through the school year. We also exchanged home addresses so if we should choose to use the *snail mail* we would know how to reach each other.

The flight to Chicago was uneventful and in too short a time it was over.

Josh claimed his luggage from the flight turntable and I waited with him. His folks were there and welcomed him home. "Mom, Dad, this is Sam, a friend from camp. Her flight to Cedar Rapids won't be in for a while. Do you mind if we wait with her before leaving for home?"

"That's fine, Josh. We're glad to meet you, Sam. Josh has mentioned you in his letters from camp. Why don't we go down to your concourse and just wait there. If you kids would like to get something to eat, there's a deli right in that area."

"Thanks, Mr. and Mrs. Cummins. I'm glad to meet you, too. Josh and I had a great week at camp and I know he'll be eager to tell you all about it."

Josh and I took off for the deli while Mr. and Mrs. Cummins took Josh's luggage and sat down in the waiting area.

I only wanted a bagel and an orange juice, while Josh ate a burger and fries and a coke.

"Sam, this has been a great week, and I know I'm going to miss you. I know you'll miss me, too, but we will keep in touch. I want to give you something that will help you remember our great times together. You remember when we were in the cave? Well, I dug out some of the clay that was on the walls and floor, and I made this for you." He handed me an exquisite little clay horse. He had molded it from the clay and it had dried perfectly. It was a perfect memento of a perfect week.

Once again I could feel the tears starting to flow, but this time there was no darkness to hide them. Josh reached over and tenderly wiped them away and said, "I won't ever forget you. Hey, it's been fun."

The End